Fantastic Folk Tales

THE SALT IN THE SEA

Norwegian Folk Tale

An imprint of Om Books International

Once there were two brothers who lived in a seaside village in Norway. The elder brother was very rich and the younger brother was very poor. One day, the younger brother realised that there was no food in the house on Christmas Eve. He decided to ask for his elder brother's help.

The evil elder brother said, "I will give you this whole turkey, only if you do something for me." The younger brother agreed.

The elder brother then said, "Take this turkey and go straight to Hell."

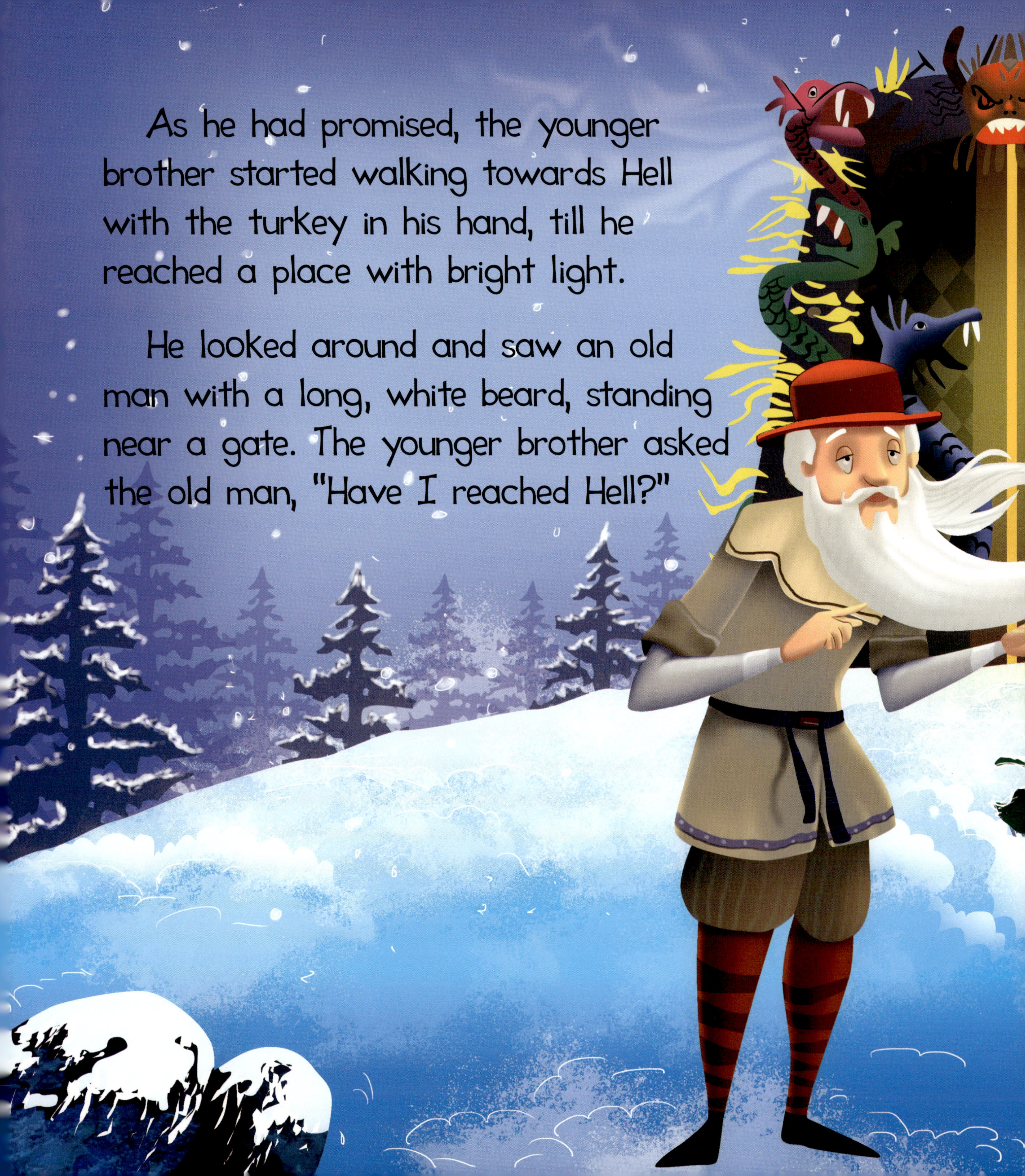

As he had promised, the younger brother started walking towards Hell with the turkey in his hand, till he reached a place with bright light.

He looked around and saw an old man with a long, white beard, standing near a gate. The younger brother asked the old man, "Have I reached Hell?"

The old man replied, "Yes, you have. Do you see that gate? That is the gate to Hell. Once you enter it, you will meet the devils. Give them the turkey, but make sure you take a hand mill from them in return. Come back to me and I will tell you how to use it."

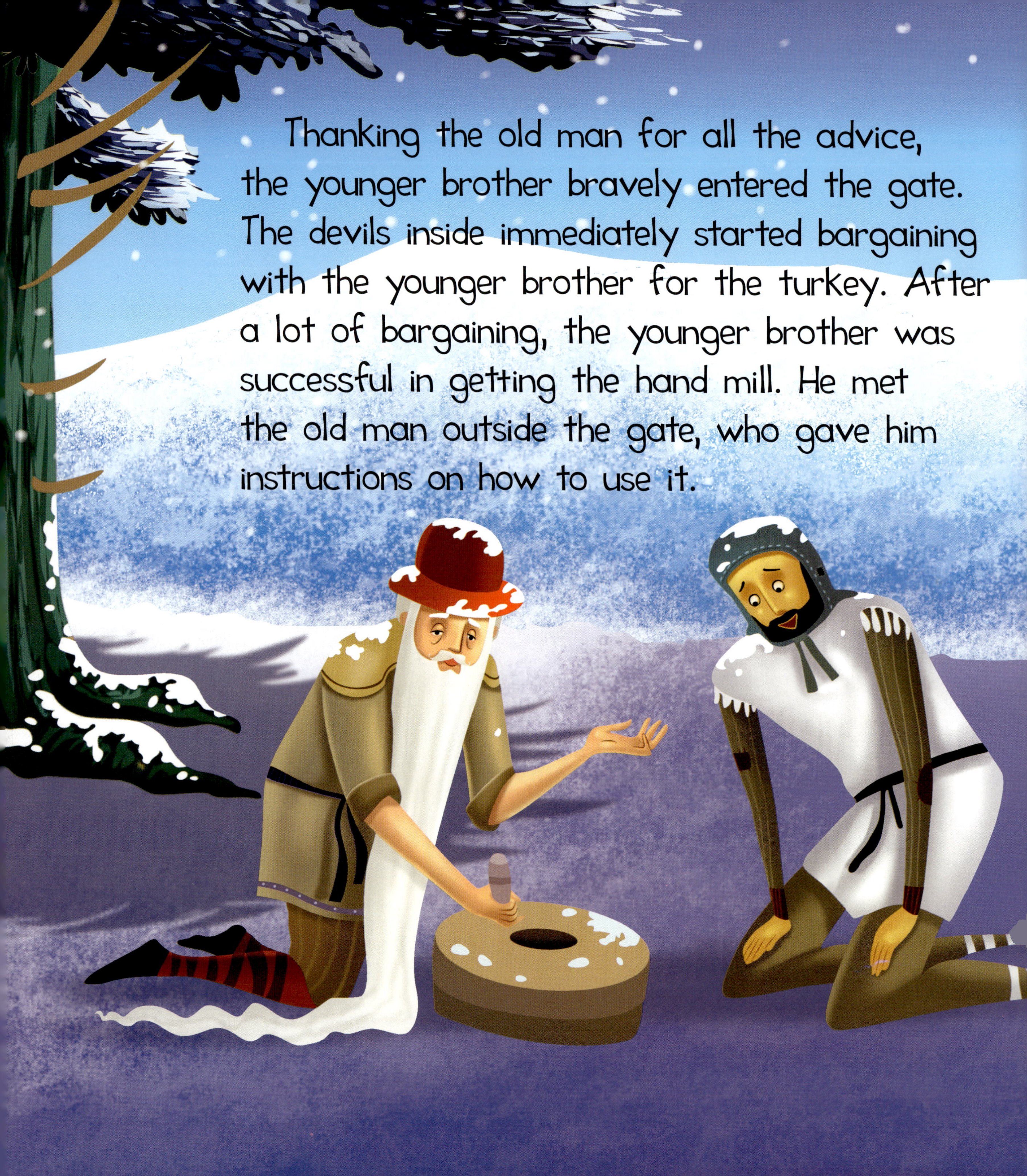

Thanking the old man for all the advice, the younger brother bravely entered the gate. The devils inside immediately started bargaining with the younger brother for the turkey. After a lot of bargaining, the younger brother was successful in getting the hand mill. He met the old man outside the gate, who gave him instructions on how to use it.

The younger brother returned home, and happily showed the hand mill to his wife. Following the instructions of the old man, the younger brother ordered the hand mill to produce food, clothes and gold coins. The wife was very happy.

They decided to throw a huge Christmas party for their family and friends. The elder brother was surprised and jealous to see his younger brother's fortune.

He found his younger brother drunk and asked him, "How did you manage to throw such a party, dear brother?" The younger brother replied, "Oh! I went to Hell as you instructed, and I exchanged the turkey for a magical hand mill. It can produce whatever I wish for!"

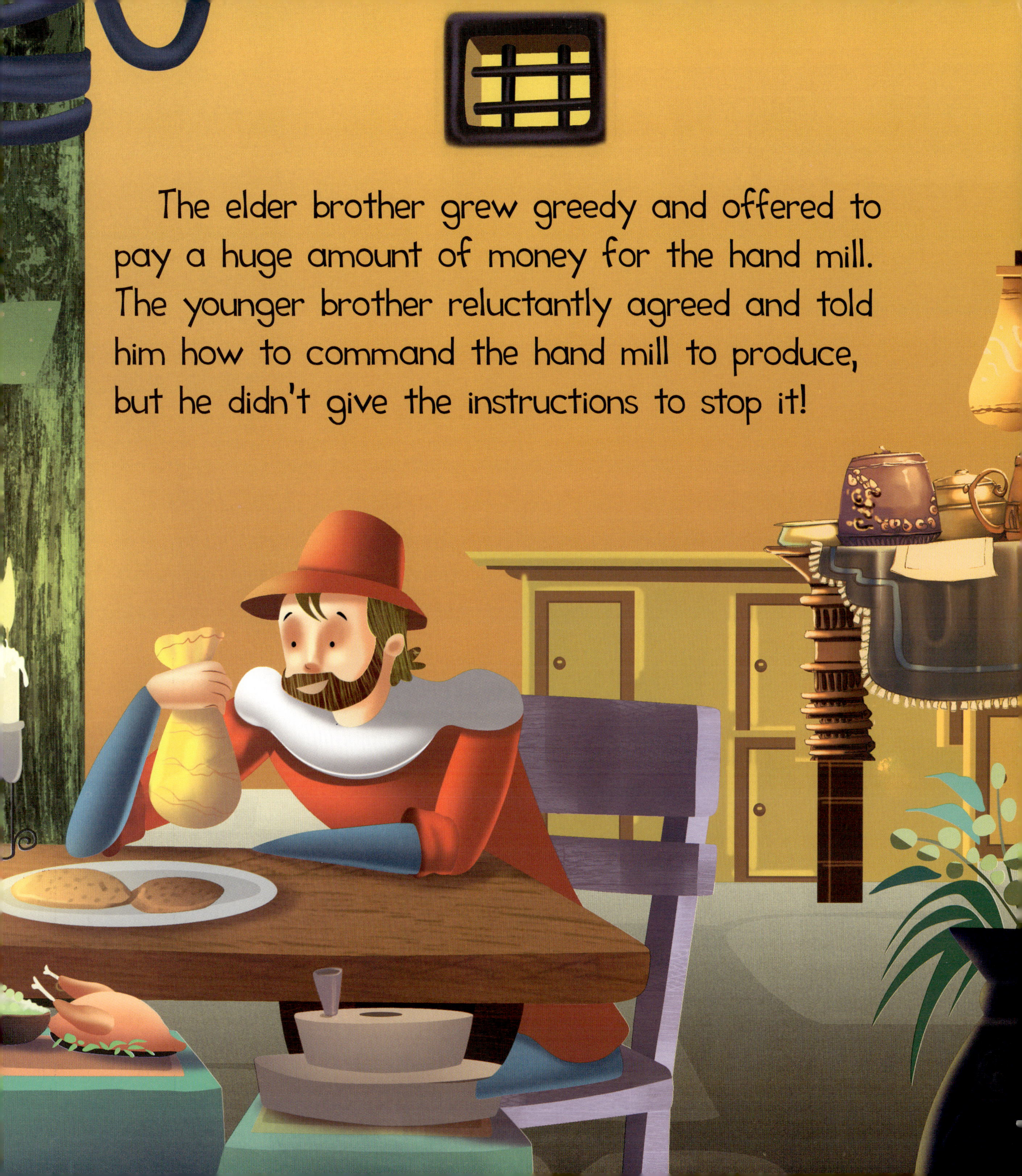

The elder brother grew greedy and offered to pay a huge amount of money for the hand mill. The younger brother reluctantly agreed and told him how to command the hand mill to produce, but he didn't give the instructions to stop it!

When the elder brother got the hand mill back home to his wife, and commanded the hand mill to produce broth, it continued to do so till the kitchen was flooded with broth. The elder brother did not know how to stop it!

The elder brother ran to his younger brother and yelled, "Help me brother, help me! This hand mill refuses to stop. It is drowning everyone and everything in all that broth!"

The younger brother replied calmly, "I will save you and your house, but you will have to give me the same amount of money you paid for the hand mill along with the hand mill." The elder brother agreed reluctantly. The younger brother used the hand mill to produce gold and food and soon became very rich. He built a huge castle for himself and settled down happily.

One day, a captain of a ship came to meet the younger brother and asked, "Can the hand mill produce salt?" The younger brother replied, "Salt? Why would you want salt?"

The captain replied, "Salt is more precious than gold as it's not readily available to people, and they pay a lot of money for even a small quantity of salt." As the younger brother was already very rich, he sold the hand mill to the captain, but he didn't give the instructions to stop the hand mill!

When the captain was far away at sea, he brought the hand mill to the deck and ordered it to produce salt. The hand mill did as it was asked. However, the captain didn't know how to stop it. Soon the ship's deck was covered in salt and the ship sank into the sea. It is believed that the hand mill is still churning salt at the bottom of the sea, which makes the sea water salty.